P9-CRB-290

MACMILLAN
Picture Wordbook

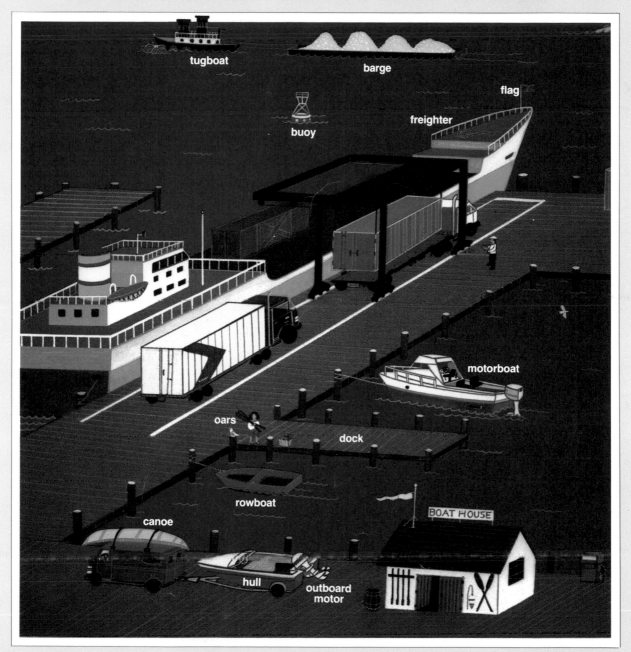

Judith S. Levey/Editor in Chief

Macmillan Publishing Company
New York

Collier Macmillan Canada
Toronto

Maxwell Macmillan International Publishing Group
New York   Oxford   Singapore   Sydney

Editorial Staff

Editor in Chief	Judith S. Levey
Managing Editor	Helen Margaret Chumbley
Editors	Deirdre Dempsey, Susan R. Norton
Production Manager	Karen L. Tates

Art Staff

Design Director	Zelda Haber
Associate Design Director	Joan Gampert
Art Director	Murray Belsky
Design	Anna Sabin
Artists	Barbara Bash, Karen Baumann, Courtney Studio, Norman Dane, Nancy Didion, Dora Leder, Susan Lexa, Frederick Marvin
Clerical Assistant	David Salinas

Pages 6–64 of this book are published in a text edition under the title
Macmillan/McGraw-Hill Picture Word Book.

**Copyright © 1990 by Macmillan Publishing Company,
a division of Maxwell Macmillan International Publishing Group**

Macmillan Publishing Company, 866 Third Avenue, New York, NY 10022
Collier Macmillan Canada, Inc., 1200 Eglinton Avenue East, Suite 200, Don Mills, Ontario M3C 3N1

First Edition

Printed in the United States of America

10 9 8 7 6 5 4 3 2 1

ISBN 0-02-754641-1

Library of Congress Cataloging-in-Publication Data

Macmillan picture wordbook / Judith S. Levey, editor in chief.—1st ed.
p.   cm.

Summary: Presents illustrated words and terms, grouped under such headings as the supermarket, outer space, clothing, and visiting the doctor.

1. Vocabulary—Juvenile literature. [1. Vocabulary.] I. Levey, Judith S., date.
PE1449.M27   1990
428.1—dc20   90-8274 CIP AC

Contents

How to Help a Child Enjoy This Book

A picture wordbook extends children's knowledge of language by showing them that words name objects—not only objects in their own environment but also those in the larger world. The **Macmillan Picture Wordbook** encourages children to investigate the world around them and offers them the vocabulary to talk about that world.

When opening the **Macmillan Picture Wordbook** for the first time, children will probably want to look quickly through all the pages, stopping when a particular picture catches their eye. This is a good time to point out some of the words that may be of interest to the children.

Listening and talking together while looking at the **Picture Wordbook** is important. Twelve characters recur throughout the book. Invite the children to find these characters in various scenes, such as In the Park, At School, Making Music, and Working with Tools.

In some of the illustrations, such as At the Supermarket, In the Home, and A Farm in the Country, objects from the main picture are shown and labeled in the margins. Not only can children see what an object looks like and learn its name, but they also can have fun finding that item in the larger picture.

Some of the colorful double-page illustrations depict familiar places and things. Others, like the Jungle or Polar Regions, give children the opportunity to explore unfamiliar environments. Children will discover plants and animals from far away, as well as those closer to home. They can view everyday people at work and at play.

4

front

back

Other activities might include asking children to plan a trip to one of the unfamiliar places shown in the book. How would they get there? What kinds of people or creatures might they encounter along the way?

Or the children might discuss what to wear at different times. What would they wear on a rainy day? Or to go to the beach? To play soccer? For travel in outer space? Have them talk about their favorite kind of weather and activity. What is the weather like today?

As children become interested in letters and sounds, the *Picture Wordbook* can be used to help them find items that start with a particular letter. Begin a game of Grandmother's Trunk by saying, "Grandmother is packing her trunk with things that begin with the letter **s**. Can you find all the things on these pages that begin with **s**?" This would be a good opportunity to introduce a child to the letters of the alphabet and to the alphabetized word list at the back of the book.

Older children may enjoy collecting their favorite words from the *Picture Wordbook* by writing them on cards. They might note all the kinds of birds, vehicles, or buildings illustrated in the book. Children may also enjoy looking at the illustration of A Family Album and then putting together a collection of snapshots or drawings of their own families.

For some children, the *Macmillan Picture Wordbook* will be their first reading book. Help children discover a love for and appreciation of language through this introduction to printed words.

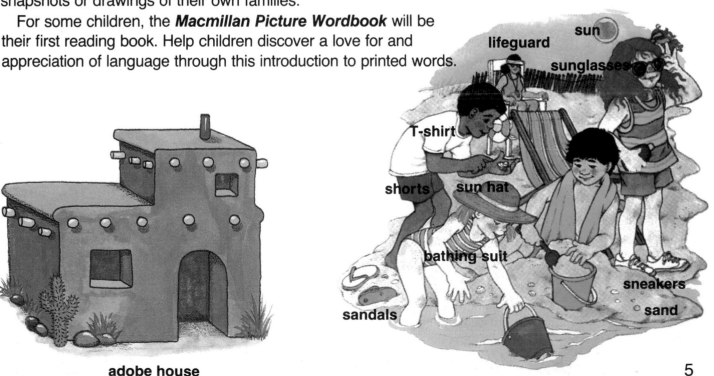

sun

lifeguard

sunglasses

T-shirt

shorts

sun hat

bathing suit

sneakers

sandals

sand

adobe house

top

bottom

on

off

up

down

out

in

IN THE PARK

grass

jungle gym

bench

slide

tunnel

tree

fountain

swings

merry-go-round

next to

in front of

behind

through

over

under

around

IN THE HOME

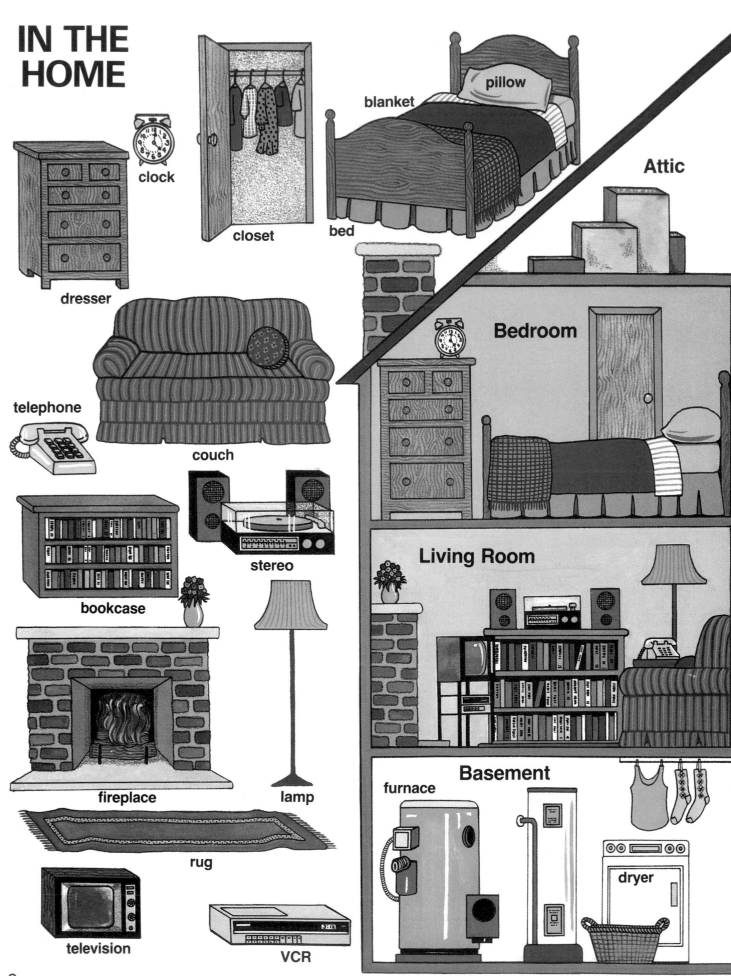

clock

closet

blanket

pillow

bed

Attic

dresser

telephone

couch

Bedroom

bookcase

stereo

fireplace

lamp

Living Room

rug

Basement

furnace

television

VCR

dryer

8

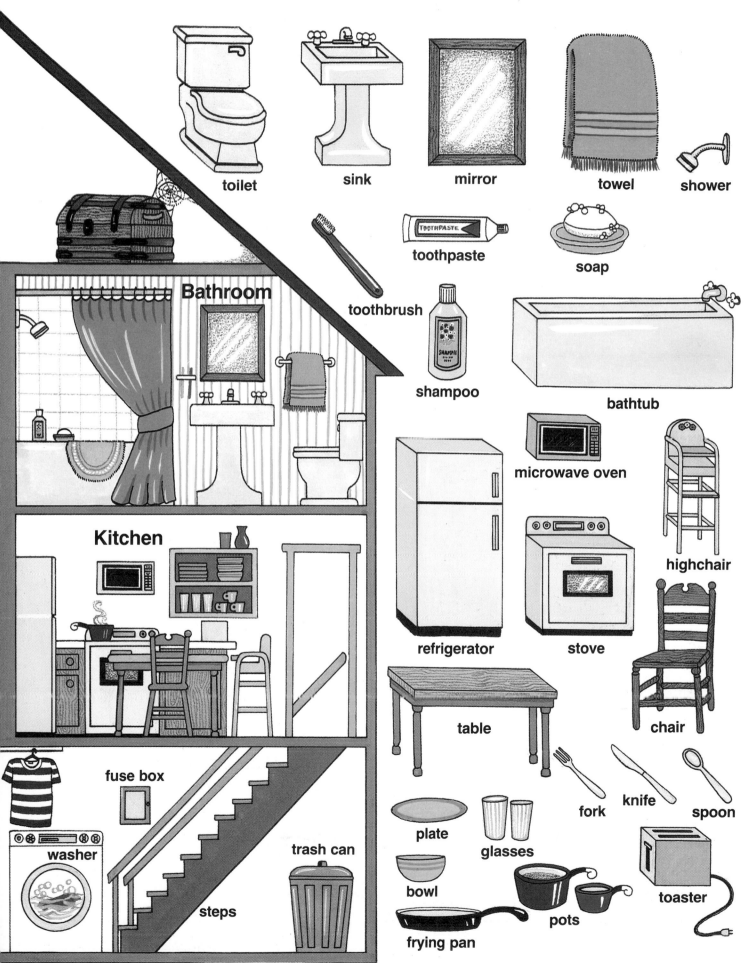

toilet

sink

mirror

towel

shower

toothpaste

soap

toothbrush

shampoo

bathtub

Bathroom

microwave oven

highchair

Kitchen

refrigerator

stove

chair

table

fuse box

fork

knife

spoon

washer

plate

glasses

trash can

bowl

toaster

steps

pots

frying pan

9

HOMES

town house

two-family house

antenna

chimney

roof

shutter

House

window

door

lawn

10

mobile home

apartment building

log cabin

tepee

house on stilts

garage

adobe house

driveway

igloo

11

AT SCHOOL

globe

headphones

tape

aquarium

easel

paintbrush

tape recorder

paints

student

paper

scissors

markers

12

bulletin board

MY CAT FLUFFY

I DON'T HAVE A PET. I HAVE A SISTER ANN.

MY DOG JEFF

clock

teacher

flag

9:00 Shared Reading
9:30 Journal Writing
10:00 Music
10:30 Recess
11:00 Individual Activities

chalkboard

A

apple

B b boat

C c cat

D d dog

chalk

eraser

OCTOBER

calendar

book

computer

table

chair

abacus

paste

pencil sharpener

crayons

pencil

13

AT THE SUPERMARKET

bread

rice

cereal

chicken

meat

fish

spices

cheese

milk

apples

eggs

oranges

grapes

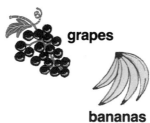
bananas

lemons

tomatoes

lettuce

carrots

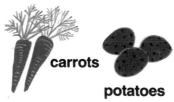
potatoes

MEAT & POULTRY

EMPLOYEES ONLY

BAKERY

FRUITS VEGETABLES

SUPERMARKET

IN

OUT

TUNA FISH 79¢ EACH

SALE

RECYCLE CANS

shopping cart

shopper

cash register

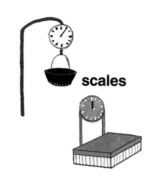

scales

clerk

checkout counter

canned food

paper towels

pet food

broccoli

corn

string beans

peanut butter

jelly

tissues

A FARM IN THE COUNTRY

dog

hay

hoe

pitchfork

pump

pail

pickup truck

weather vane

scarecrow

fence

plow

tractor

pigpen

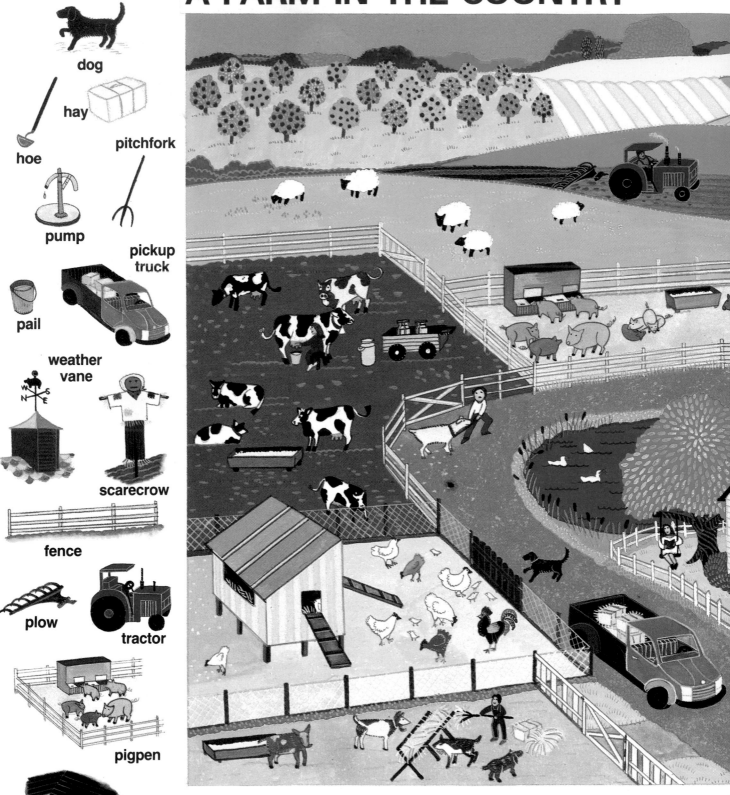

porch

hayloft

chicken coop

garden

rooster

hen

chicks

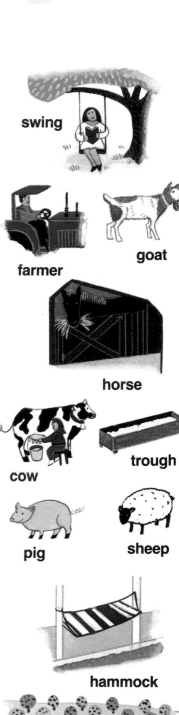

swing

farmer

goat

horse

cow

trough

pig

sheep

hammock

orchard

field

cat

ducks

windmill

farmhouse

pasture

silo

barn

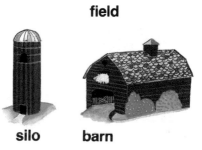

17

IN THE CITY

restaurant and café

waiter

museum

fruit and vegetable stand

dry cleaner

newsstand

firehouse

traffic light
bicycle messenger
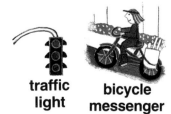

bus

coffee shop

mail carrier
hot dog stand

apartment building

bank

street light

school

subway

skyscraper

telephone booth

department store

police officer

taxicab

parking garage

bus stop

church

parking meter

post office

hospital

library

mailbox

bookstore

movie theater

fire hydrant

19

grasshopper

butterfly

herd

gazelle

rhinoceros

ostrich

hyena

flowers

leopard

vines

parrot

monkey

gorilla

toucan

tiger

ferns

JUNGLE

20

AFRICAN PLAIN

giraffes

secretary bird

hippopotamus

zebras

grass

vulture

jackal

lion

elephants

chimpanzee

boa constrictor

DESERT

cactus

mule deer

fox

roadrunner

coyote

jackrabbit

burrow

gila monster

rattlesnake

lizard

spider

mouse

scorpion

22

peak

MOUNTAINS

valley

eagle

bighorn
sheep

mountain
goats

waterfall

stream

mountain lion

bear

wildflowers

moss

cave

bats

23

leaves

owl

acorns

raccoon

oak tree

pine

pine cones

FOREST

branch

porcupine

woodpecker

deer

birch

opossum

rabbit

moose

trunk

violets

skunk

mushrooms

squirrel

chipmunk

caterpillar

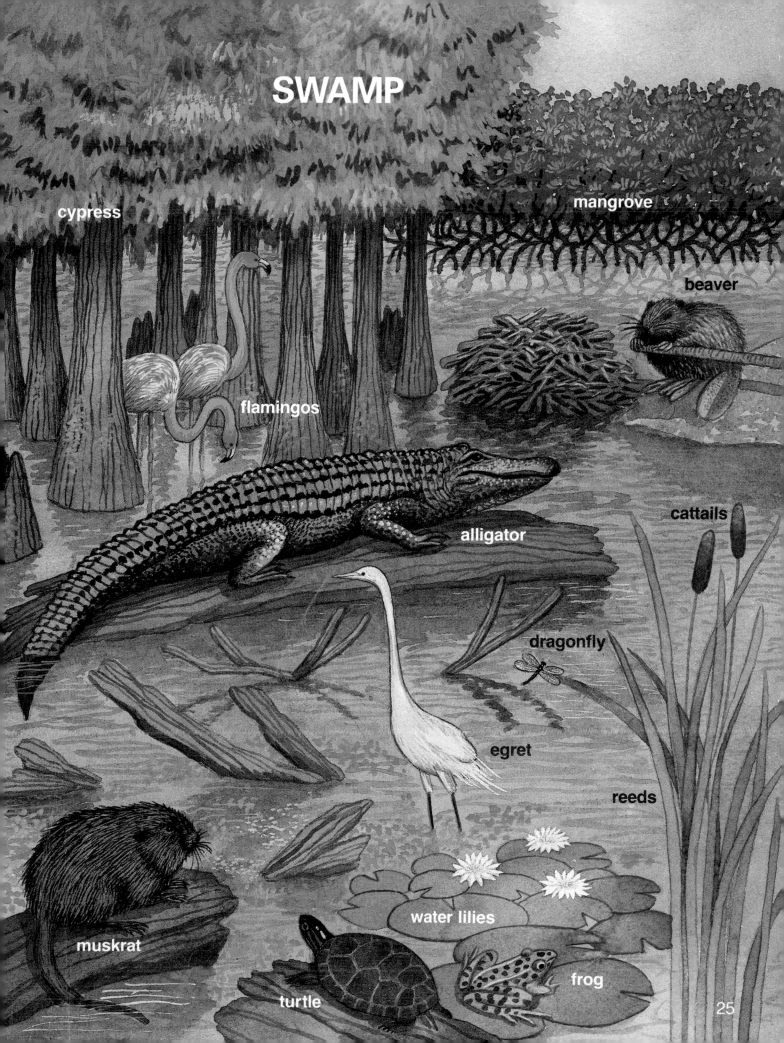

SWAMP

cypress

mangrove

flamingos

beaver

alligator

cattails

dragonfly

egret

reeds

muskrat

water lilies

turtle

frog

POLAR REGIONS

musk ox

reindeer

walruses

ice and snow

ermine

snowy owl

arctic fox

polar bear

arctic hares

sea urchins

turtle

dolphin

sea horse

jellyfish

tuna

26

sky

flying fish

penguins

seals

ocean

crab

starfish

barnacles

mussels

sponges

sea anemone

seaweed

coral

lobster

octopus

eel

swordfish

manta ray

whale

UNDER THE SEA

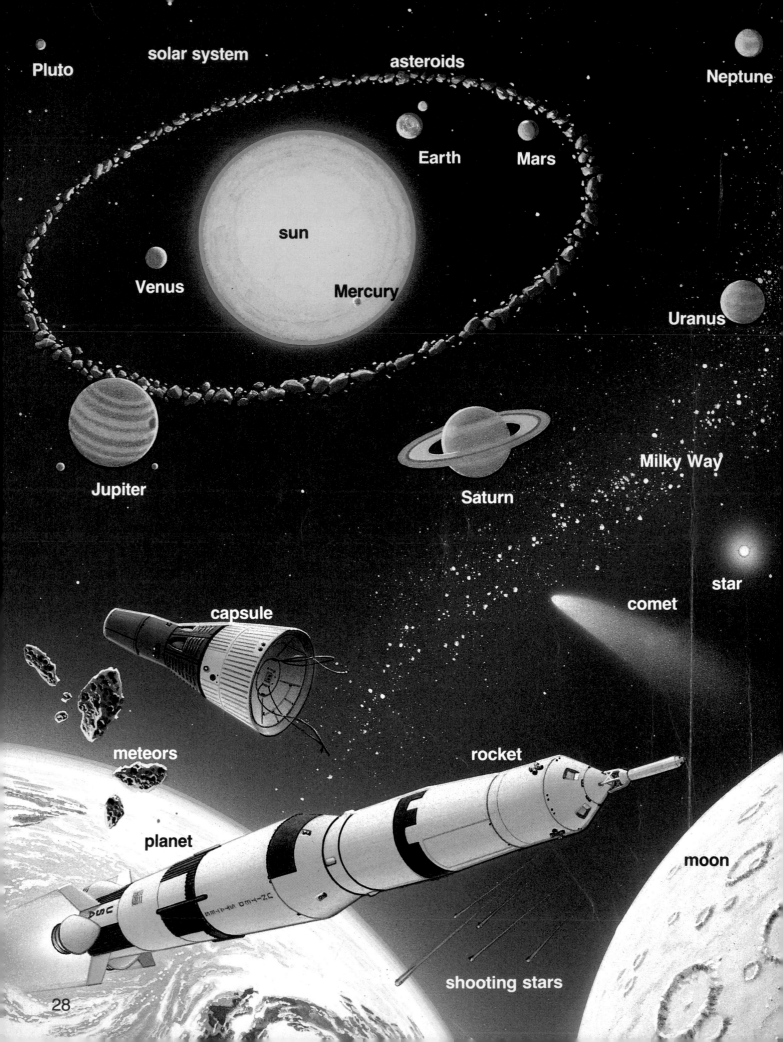

Pluto

solar system

asteroids

Neptune

Earth

Mars

sun

Venus

Mercury

Uranus

Jupiter

Milky Way

Saturn

star

capsule

comet

meteors

rocket

planet

moon

shooting stars

28

OUTER SPACE

space stations

satellite

spacesuit

lunar module

astronaut

space shuttle

29

SPRING

hill

flying a kite

hiking

playing baseball

pond

ducks

fishing

mowing the grass

jogging

riding a bicycle

roller-skating

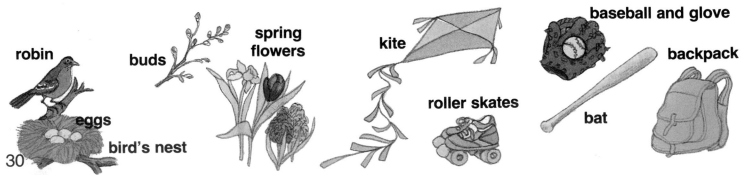

robin

buds

spring flowers

kite

baseball and glove

backpack

roller skates

bat

eggs

bird's nest

SUMMER

playing tennis

rowing a boat

watering the flowers

SWIM AREA

playing volleyball

swimming

inner tube

net

having a picnic

picnic basket

picnic table

jumping rope

climbing a tree

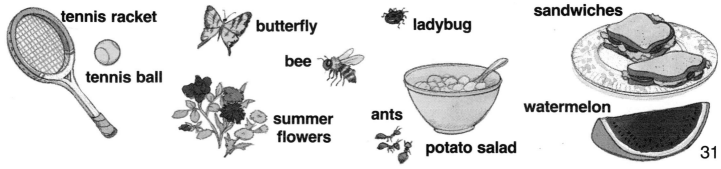

tennis racket

butterfly

ladybug

sandwiches

tennis ball

bee

summer flowers

ants

potato salad

watermelon

FALL

playing soccer

hay · going on a hayride

wagon

raking leaves

picking apples

carving pumpkins

ladder

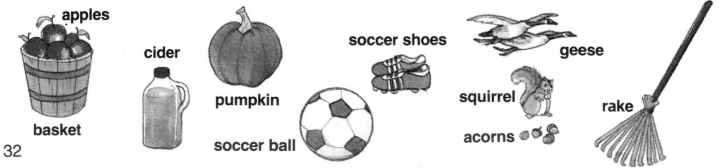

apples

cider

pumpkin

soccer shoes

geese

squirrel

acorns

rake

basket

soccer ball

WINTER

skiing

sledding

holly bush

playing ice hockey

shoveling snow

ice

bird feeder

ice-skating

making a snowman

making snow angels

evergreen tree

making snowballs

sled

ski poles

skis

ice skates

hockey stick

hockey puck

cardinal

sparrows

icicles

holly leaves and berries

33

CLOTHES WE WEAR

cloud

umbrella

rain

rain hat

raincoat

poncho

rain boots

puddle

A Rainy Day

sun

lifeguard

sunglasses

T-shirt

sun hat

shorts

bathing suit

sandals

sneakers

sand

A Sunny Day

cap

sweater

jacket

dress

pajamas

jeans

pants

socks

34

snow

earmuffs

hat

mittens

scarf

gloves

snowsuit

snowman

parka

snow boots

A Snowy Day

skirt

nightgown

slippers

coat

sweatshirt

sweatpants

suspenders

shoes

shirt

35

AT THE AIRPORT

runway

cockpit

cabin

jet engine

Airplane

tail

wing

nose

NEWSSTAND

RESTAURANT

baggage truck

flight attendants

gate

waiting area

check-in counter

GATE 5

boarding ramp

control tower

mechanic

baggage compartment

landing gear

pilot

passengers

observation
area

GIFT SHOP

arrival and departure
monitors

ticket
agent

GATES
5-10

rest rooms

INFORMATION

ticket
counter

information desk

baggage
carousel 275

security check

metal detector

boarding pass

garment
bag

carry-on
luggage

skycap

baggage
cart

suitcases

37

TRAINS

tunnel

tank car

steam locomotive

livestock car

switch tower

caboose

Rio Grande

4065

dining car

passenger car

diesel locomotive

railroad crossing

traffic signal

rail switch

crossing gate

bench

engineer

passengers

conductor

porter

trestle

refrigerator car

automobile car

·L·G·B· 4059

flatcar

boxcar

D&RGW 4060

2GD

76

sleeping car

2 67

TICKETS
MAP
TRAIN STATION
TAXI

COFFEE

TAXI

platform

train
signal

TICKETS

tracks

TAXI

stationmaster

waiting room

ticket window

ties

rails

taxi
station

tugboat

barge

buoy

flag

freighter

lifeboat

container truck

motorboat

oars

dock

rowboat

canoe

BOAT HOUSE

hull

outboard motor

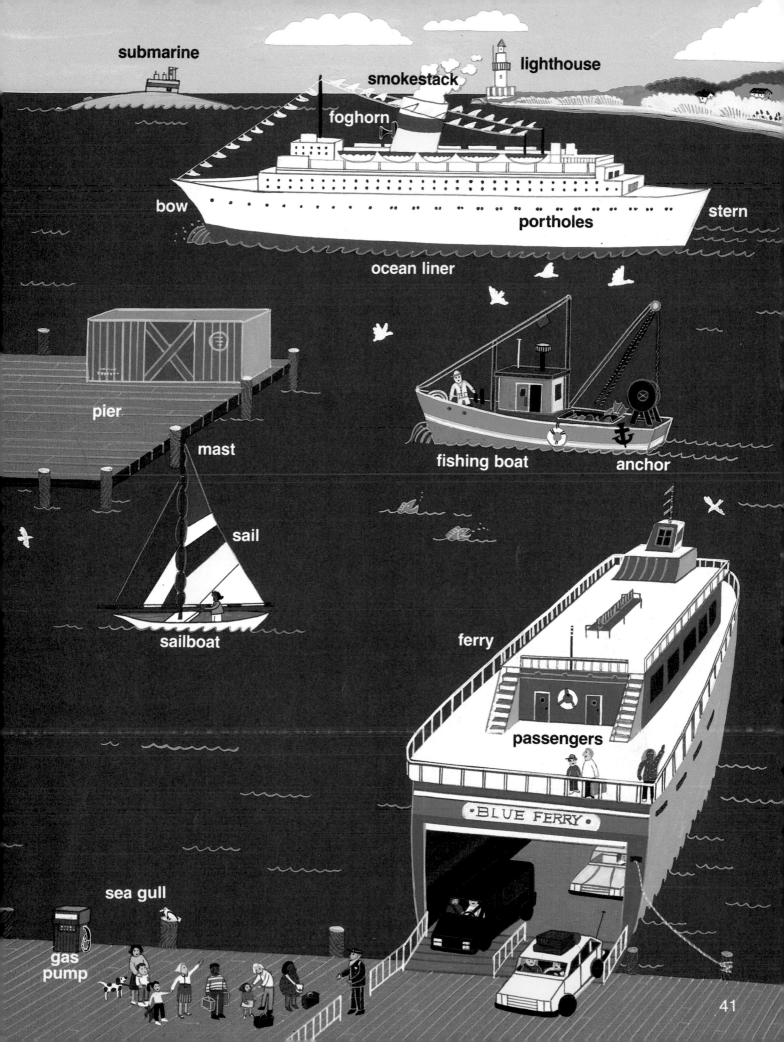

submarine

smokestack

lighthouse

foghorn

bow

portholes

stern

ocean liner

pier

mast

fishing boat

anchor

sail

sailboat

ferry

passengers

·BLUE FERRY·

sea gull

gas pump

41

GOING PLACES

trailer truck

PAY TOLL 1 MILE

SPEED LIMIT 30

car

school bus

bus

ONE WAY

STOP

SCHOOL CROSSING

NO PARKING

fire engine

DO NOT ENTER

NO U TURN

jeep

van

camper

double-decker bus

minivan

DEAD END

STEEP HILL

garbage truck

moving van

EXIT

tank truck

station wagon

NO LEFT TURN

mail truck

U.S. MAIL

GON-102

ambulance

AMBULANCE

SLIPPERY WHEN WET

tow truck

convertible

TAW-117

motorcycle

road

AT A CONSTRUCTION SITE

beam

crane

girder

scaffold

ladder

lumber

forklift

electrical cables

jackhammer

hand truck

44

wrenches

saw

hacksaw

try square

level

hammer

masking tape

safety knife

hand drill

stapler

coping saw

sledgehammer

vise

sawhorse

tool box

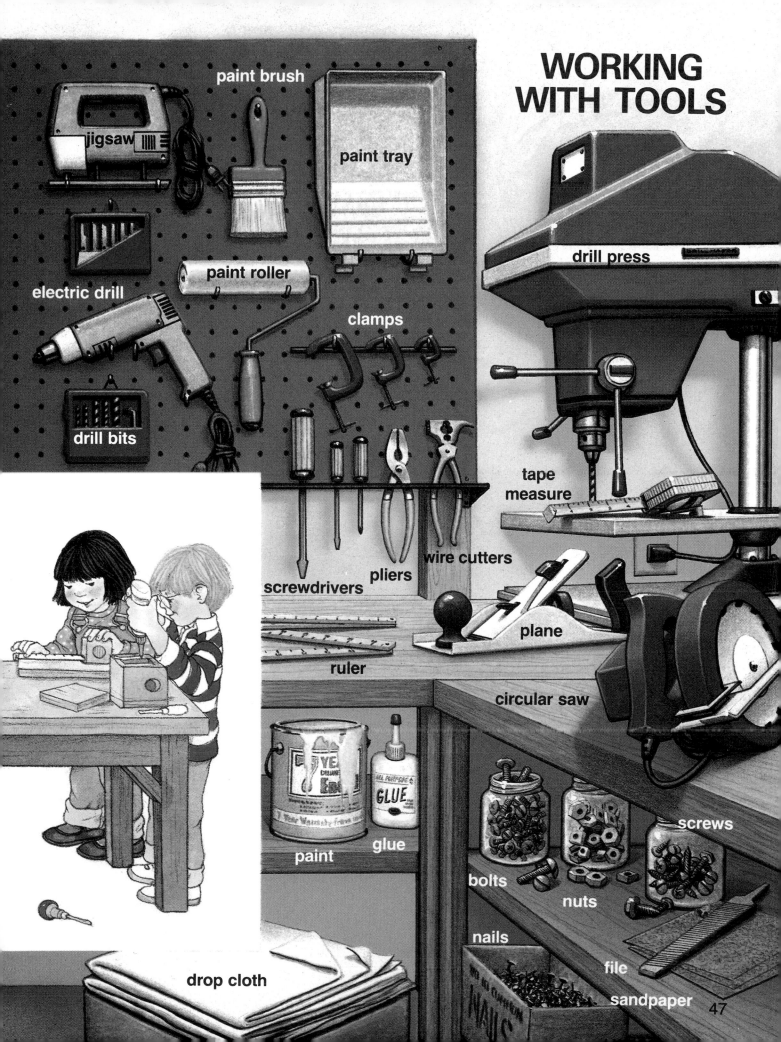

WORKING WITH TOOLS

paint brush

paint tray

jigsaw

electric drill

paint roller

drill bits

drill press

clamps

tape measure

screwdrivers

pliers

wire cutters

plane

ruler

circular saw

paint

glue

bolts

nuts

screws

nails

drop cloth

file

sandpaper

47

MAKING MUSIC

harp

triangle

Chorus

piano

sheet music

singer

bagpipe

maracas

tambourine

trombone

guitar

harmonica

saxophone

xylophone

48

Orchestra

cymbals

tuba

clarinet

French horn

baton

oboe

bass

violin

trumpet

flute

conductor

music stand

cello

recorder

bugle

piccolo

accordion

drum

49

A FAMILY ALBUM

me

my mother and father

my sister and brother

my mother and her parents

my grandmother and grandfather and me

my mother and her brother

my uncle and me

my dog Winky

my father and his sister

my aunt, her daughter and son, and their stepfather

my parents and their niece and nephew

my cousins and me

all of us ♡

VISITING THE DOCTOR

doctor

stethoscope

scale

cotton balls

gauze pads

tongue depressors

bandages

bulb syringe

tweezers

thermometer

blood pressure cuff

nurse

patient

doctor's bag

examining table

52

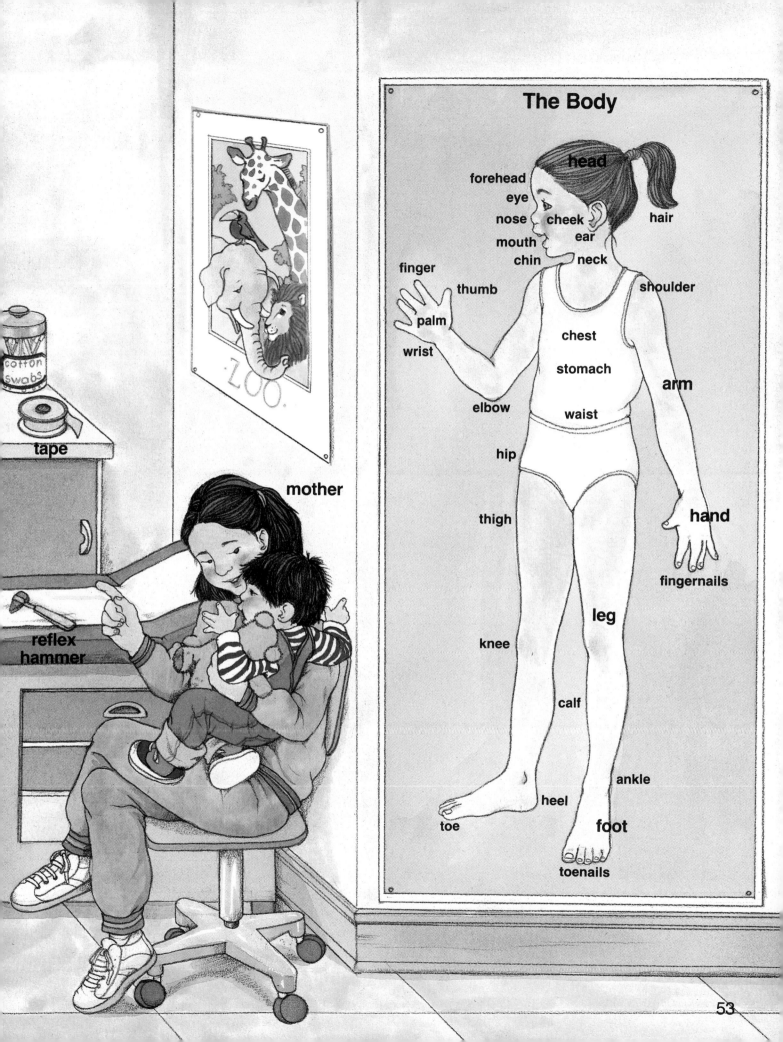

The Body

head
forehead
eye
nose
cheek
hair
mouth
ear
chin
neck
finger
thumb
shoulder
palm
chest
wrist
stomach
arm
elbow
waist
hip
thigh
hand
fingernails
leg
knee
calf
ankle
heel
toe
foot
toenails

cotton swabs
tape
reflex hammer
mother

THE WORLD OF FANTASY

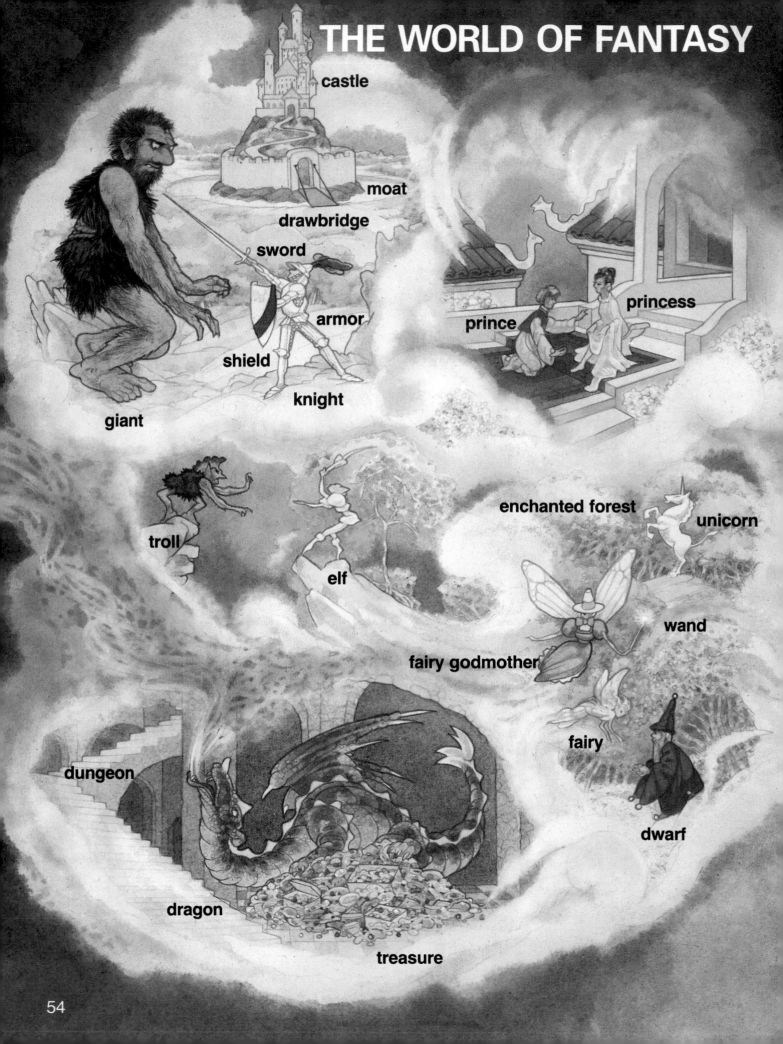

castle

moat

drawbridge

sword

armor

shield

knight

giant

prince

princess

troll

elf

enchanted forest

unicorn

wand

fairy godmother

fairy

dungeon

dwarf

dragon

treasure

flags

crow's nest

sails

pirate ship

magic carpet

genie

crown

king

queen

wizard

staff

lamp

NUMBERS, OPPOSITES, AND SHAPES

1 one
2 two
3 three
4 four
5 five
6 six
7 seven
8 eight
9 nine
10 ten

many

tall

short

few

high

low

narrow

wide

small

large

soft

hard

closed

open

full

empty

front

back

circle

triangle

square

crescent

rectangle

diamond

star

57

THE ALPHABET
AND COLORS

white

pink

red

orange

yellow

Aa Bb

Cc Dd Ee Ff

Gg Hh Ii Jj Kk

Ll Mm Nn Oo

Pp Qq Rr Ss

Tt Uu Vv Ww

Xx Yy Zz

green   blue   purple   brown   gray   black

WORD LIST